Bree's Crib

CATHERINE MALASKI • LISA PERRETT

Gram set me in my crib.

It is time to nap,
Bree.

I drop my crab
from my crib.

I drag my frog
from side to side.

I drive my truck up
on top.

I grip my crib.

Grab me, Fred!

Gram, I am up!

No nap for me.

Time to drum
with Fred.

BANG!
BANG!

Phonics Focus Words: Beginning r-blends

Bree('s)	drop	grab
crab	drum	Gram
crib	Fred	grip
drag	frog	truck
drive		

Decodable Words

am	nap	side
bang	no	time
in	on	top
it	set	up
me		

High-Frequency Words

for	is	to
from	my	with
I		